We Are Brothers, We Are Friends

Alexandra Penfold   Pictures by Eda Kaban

Farrar Straus Giroux

New York

For my favorite pair of brothers —A.P.

For my husband, Dax. Always —E.K.

Farrar Straus Giroux Books for Young Readers
175 Fifth Avenue, New York 10010

Text copyright © 2017 by Alexandra Penfold
Pictures copyright © 2017 by Eda Kaban
All rights reserved
Color separations by Embassy Graphics
Printed in China by Toppan Leefung Printing Ltd.,
Dongguan City, Guangdong Province
Designed by Kristie Radwilowicz
First edition, 2017
1   3   5   7   9   10   8   6   4   2

mackids.com

Library of Congress Cataloging-in-Publication Data

Names: Penfold, Alexandra, author. | Kaban, Eda, illustrator.
Title: We are brothers, we are friends / Alexandra Penfold ; pictures by Eda
    Kaban.
Description: First edition. | New York : Farrar Straus Giroux, 2017. |
    Summary: "A brother explains to his new baby brother all the fun adventures
    they will have together because they are brothers and friends"— Provided by
    publisher.
Identifiers: LCCN 2016001912 | ISBN 9780374302016 (hardback)
Subjects: | CYAC: Babies—Fiction. | Brothers—Fiction. | BISAC: JUVENILE
    FICTION / Family / New Baby. | JUVENILE FICTION / Family / Siblings. |
    JUVENILE FICTION / Social Issues / New Experience.
Classification: LCC PZ7.1.P446 We 2017 | DDC [E]—dc23
LC record available at https://lccn.loc.gov/2016001912

Our books may be purchased in bulk for promotional, educational, or business use. Please
contact your local bookseller or the Macmillan Corporate and Premium Sales Department
at (800) 221-7945 ext. 5442 or by e-mail at MacmillanSpecialMarkets@macmillan.com.

We are brothers. We are friends.

I'm the big brother.
You're just little. But that's okay.
I have lots to show you . . .

like trains

and planes

and how to be a dinosaur.

We will have adventures,

just the two of us.

I will teach you to laugh.

I will teach you to sing.

I will teach you about hiding

and seeking.

When you cry . . .

Don't worry, baby.
I will help!

I will give you gentle pats
and kiss your little toesies.

I will share my best toys

and my mama
and my dada, too.

We are brothers.
We are friends.

And we will have adventures, just the two of us.